TEENAGE MUTANT NINJA TURTLES

THE RISE OF TIGER CLAW

Published in the United States by Random House Children's Books, a
division of Penguin Random House LLC, 1745 Broadway, New York,
NY 10019, and in Canada by Random House of Canada, a division of
Penguin Random House Ltd., Toronto. Random House and the colophon
are registered trademarks of Penguin Random House LLC. Nickelodeon,
Teenage Mutant Ninja Turtles, and all related titles, logos, and characters
are trademarks of Viacom International Inc. and Viacom Overseas Holdings
C.V. Based on characters created by Peter Laird and Kevin Eastman.

randomhousekids.com

ISBN 978-0-553-52274-7

Printed in the United States of America
10 9 8 7 6 5 4 3 2

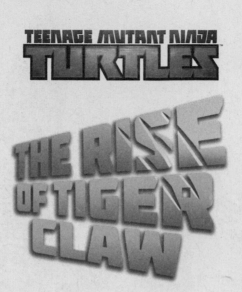

TEENAGE MUTANT NINJA TURTLES

THE RISE OF TIGER CLAW

Adapted by David Lewman

Based on the teleplay "Wormquake!"
by Brandon Auman and John Shirley

RANDOM HOUSE 🏠 NEW YORK

The ninja warriors of the Foot Clan crouched behind a billboard on top of a New York City skyscraper. They were hunting the Turtles.

"Karai," Rahzar snarled. "Shredder didn't authorize your little operation. I think we should—"

Karai turned, sharply cutting him off. "Silence," she hissed. "*I'm* in charge while my father's in Japan! If we score an ambush on the Turtles, it'll make us *both* look good! Now quiet . . . here they come."

Leonardo, Michelangelo, Donatello, and Raphael quickly leaped and flipped from rooftop to rooftop. Suddenly, Leo signaled for them to stop.

"Hold up, ninjas!" he said quietly. "I have the feeling we're not alone."

"You're right, Leo," Mikey agreed, looking around. "We have a potential *spy*!" He darted over to a wall and put his face close to . . . a squirrel! Startled, the squirrel dropped its acorn and ran off. Mikey grinned.

"Shhh!" Donnie warned. "I thought I heard—"

"FOOT! ATTACK!" ordered Karai from atop a brick shaft. Swinging their weapons, the Footbots and Rahzar ran straight at the Teenage Mutant Ninja Turtles!

Rahzar leaped at Michelangelo, his long fangs and sharp claws ready for impact, and knocked him to the ground.

"Serving one bot, hot!" Raph shouted as he whacked a Footbot with his *sai*. Leo used his *katana* swords to fight off two other deadly Footbots.

"Get off me, Rahzar!" Mikey yelled as the mutant inched his fatal fangs closer to the Turtle's face. *WHAP!* Donnie knocked Rahzar off Mikey with his trusty *bo* staff! Mikey gave Donnie a quick but grateful fist bump.

Karai couldn't resist joining the fight herself. She leaped down from her perch, facing off against Raphael and Leonardo. They raised their weapons. "Let's take her down!" Raph cried, eagerly spinning his *sais*. "Once and for all!" He'd fought Karai before and was sick of her interference.

But taking Karai down wouldn't be easy. As a highly trained *kunoichi,* or female ninja, she was quick, strong, and ruthless. She knocked Raph back with her blade as soon as he attacked her. Just then, another Footbot jumped in and took all of Raph's attention. It was up to Leo to deal with Karai.

He leaped and swung his *katana* swords, but Leo didn't want to just fight Karai. He had something important to tell her. "Karai, listen!" he called.

Karai ignored him, figuring the Turtle was trying to distract her. She kept on leaping and running, dodging Leo's blows and swinging her sword. She raised it high over her head and tried to slam it down on Leo, but he crossed his swords and blocked her. As Leo balanced on the roof's ledge, the two fighters struggled against each other, inches apart.

"There's something you should know!" Leo said. "It's about your father!"

Karai's eyes widened in surprise and anger. *How dare this mutant speak of my father?* she thought. She gave a mighty push and sent Leo over the edge of the rooftop.

He fell past two tall brick chimneys, back-flipped in the air, and landed on his feet. He was on the next roof over. "Your real father!" he called up to Karai.

She leaped down and swung her sword, using the force of her fall to crash her weapon into Leo's. He skidded backward across the roof, his *katana*

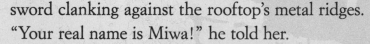

sword clanking against the rooftop's metal ridges. "Your real name is Miwa!" he told her.

Karai glared at Leo. "I'm not interested in anything but you begging for your life!"

As she ran toward him to deliver a punishing strike, the whole building began to shake! Karai hesitated, struggling to stay on her feet.

The other Turtles, still on the building where the

fight began, felt the shaking, too. "Whoa!" Mikey yelled, trying to keep his balance. "Earthquake!"

"In New York?" Rahzar said. None of them could remember an earthquake happening in New York.

The huge brick chimney behind Karai started to crack and fall from the violent shaking. "Karai, look out!" Leo shouted. He jumped forward to push her out of the way. She swung her sword at him, but he managed to shove her to safety.

Now, the whole chimney was coming down! Leo tried to outrun the falling tower, but he wasn't fast enough. Leo was buried under a massive pile of bricks!

CHAPTER 2

Donnie, Raph, and Mikey dug frantically through the pile of bricks, searching for their brother. "Leo!" Mikey called, hoping for an answer.

Finally, they saw the edge of a blue mask. "Leo?" Mikey said again.

Leonardo shook himself and looked at his brothers. "Ugh," he groaned. "I think my shell got knocked loose."

His brothers grinned. Leo was alive!

"What was that shaking?" Leo asked.

"Some kind of localized quake," Donnie guessed. "But what caused it?"

Leo stood up and glanced around. "What happened to the Footbots? And Rahzar? And Karai?"

"They took off when the shaking started," Raphael said.

"Yeah, right!" Mikey said, nodding and smiling. "The shaking scared them off. Or maybe they saw they were getting their butts kicked, so they ran away!"

What the Turtles didn't know was that Rahzar had disapproved of Karai's plan from the beginning. When the shaking began, he saw a good opportunity to abandon the mission. The Footbots followed him, and Karai, finding herself outnumbered, had seen no option but to join the retreat.

Leo looked strangely disappointed that their enemies had left. "Aw, no," he said. "She's gone! I could have changed everything!" He hung his head and closed his eyes. "Now it's too late. . . ."

His brothers looked at each other. What was Leo talking about?

Back in their secret headquarters deep below the streets of New York, Mikey and Raph watched news reporter Carlos Chiang O'Brien talk about the earthquake on TV.

"Scientists are calling them microquakes," he said, "but they shook so hard this reporter's hair was badly messed up!" His hair looked wild, like a family of snakes. He ran his hand over his head to smooth it down. "No need for concern," he added seriously. "I'm being treated by my stylist."

Mikey was shocked. "Dude! His poor hair!"

Raph shot his brother a sideways glance. "Earthquakes in Manhattan?" he murmured to himself. "Something is definitely up!"

He and Mikey went looking for Donnie, who was busy in his lab. He showed them a map of New York City on a computer screen, with red dots moving toward a central point. "I've been graphing the earthquake epicenters," Donnie explained. "They're happening in a pattern that's not at all random."

Mikey was confused. "Is that awesome good or awesome bad?"

"Awesome *bad,* Mikey," Donnie said, frowning. He tapped the keys of his computer. "I've got weird energy readings under the epicenter. I think some kind of *tech* is causing the quakes."

Raph looked at Donnie. "Huh. Are you thinking what I'm thinking?"

Mikey stared at Raph, thinking about a cute kitty with big eyes.

Raph made an exasperated sound and whacked Mikey in the head. "Ow!" Mikey cried, his eyes spinning.

Raph put his fists on his hips and tried to guide Mikey to the answer he was thinking of. "Mikey, who has that kind of technology?"

"Hmm," Mikey said, thinking hard. He imagined two cute kittens playing with a screwdriver.

In the lair's *dojo,* the Teenage Mutant Ninja Turtles' sensei, Splinter, sat under the chamber's gnarled tree, meditating.

Leo stood in the doorway, working up the

courage to enter and tell his teacher what he had done. He was not looking forward to Splinter's reaction.

He walked in and knelt on the carpet. "Master Splinter," he said quietly. "I tried to tell Karai . . . that you're her father."

Splinter opened his eyes, surprised by Leo's confession. He grunted his disapproval.

Leo didn't like the sound of that grunt, but he hurried on, getting out all the words he had carefully planned to say. "I thought if she knew, she might come over to our side."

Splinter grunted again. He stood, put his hands behind his back.

"There is a saying," Splinter said. "He who runs his mouth gets a face full of *nunchaku.*"

Leo knew very well that *nunchaku* was another word for *nunchucks,* but he had never heard that saying. "They say that in Japan?" he asked.

"They would if *you* were there!" Splinter answered. He thought for a moment. "Still," he continued, "your heart is in the right place." He closed his eyes, then opened them wide. "Perhaps it is time she knew the truth."

"Maybe," Leo suggested cautiously, "you should tell the other guys."

Master Splinter closed his eyes again. He knew Leonardo was right, but it didn't make hearing his words any less painful.

A few moments later, Leo brought his three brothers into the *dojo*. They knelt on the carpets, waiting to hear what Splinter had to tell them.

"This is difficult," he began, "but it is time you knew the truth. I told you once about losing my wife and my home in Japan, back when I was a man, not a . . . rat. I fought Shredder, and there was a fire. I long thought I had lost my daughter in that fire."

The brothers nodded. They remembered.

"But I was wrong," Splinter continued. "The child I thought I had lost, Miwa . . . is Karai. My daughter."

Donnie, Raph, and Mikey gasped, shocked by this news.

"In the darkness of the smoke and fire, Shredder stole Miwa away," Splinter said in a pained voice. "I thought she had perished, but she was raised by Shredder as *his* daughter. He trained her to become a deadly Foot assassin and changed her name to Karai."

For a long moment, the brothers didn't know what to say. Then Donnie stammered, "This—this can't be!"

"It's some kinda joke, right, Sensei?" Raph asked.

"Karai's our *sister*?" Mikey blurted.

Raph shook his head, unable to accept this information. "Sensei, she's still our enemy. She was raised by Shredder!" He got to his feet.

So did Donnie. "Yeah! How could we ever *trust* her?"

Master Splinter crossed the chamber and picked up an old black-and-white framed photo of himself as a man with his wife and baby daughter. He stared at the photo for the millionth time. "There is good in her. I know this."

He turned
back to his sons,
meeting their
questioning gazes.
"The truth must
be told," he said
decisively.
"And it too
will be an
earthquake."

CHAPTER 3

In another part of the city, Karai was waiting impatiently in Shredder's tall lair built of steel and glass. "Father should've been back hours ago with his new little secret weapon."

The purple mutant, Fishface, stood nervously to the side. Only Rahzar spoke up. "All I know is that he's a deadly assassin. The Kraang turned him into a mutant when he was a kid, decades ago."

At the end of the long chamber, heavy doors crashed open. Eight Footbots marched in, took their places, and bowed their heads as their master walked by.

Shredder climbed the steps and sat on his cold granite throne. "I have returned," he said in his deep menacing voice. "And I bring with me the most feared assassin in all of Asia . . . Tiger Claw!"

Karai, Rahzar, Baxter Stockman, and Fishface all turned their heads to look down the long walkway to the doors.

A tall and daunting mutant, Tiger Claw had the head and claws of a tiger but the powerful body and deep voice of a man. He wore blasters in the holsters strapped to his legs, with a bandolier of ammo across his chest. He strode past the bowing Footbots. When he reached the steps leading up to Shredder's throne, he knelt obediently on one knee.

Despite the impressive entrance, Karai refused to be cowed. "*This* is your secret weapon, Father? Another *freak*?"

Tiger Claw stood up to his full height and glanced disdainfully over his shoulder. "This is the Foot Clan you promised me?" he sneered. "I must say, Master Shredder, I am disappointed!"

Insulted, Karai drew her sword and rushed at Tiger Claw. The assassin immediately drew his blaster and wheeled on Karai, aiming it right at her head. He growled.

Fishface quickly but nervously stepped forward, hoping to break the tension. "I honor you, great Tiger Claw! Can I offer you some refreshments?"

Scowling, Tiger Claw lowered his weapon. "Milk," he rumbled. "Skim."

Fishface backed humbly out of the chamber to fetch some skim milk.

Karai noticed that Tiger Claw's striped tail was no more than a stub. "Sensitive subject maybe, but shouldn't tigers have tails?"

"Don't mock me, child," Tiger Claw warned. "It was a rival who sliced off my tail. One day I will find him . . . and he will pay the price!"

Fishface slipped back in carrying a tray with a small cup of milk. He lifted the tray to Tiger Claw, who took the cup and lapped up the milk like a giant cat, purring.

"If you can't keep your own tail—" Karai started to observe, but Shredder cut her off.

"Silence, Karai! You will treat Tiger Claw with the utmost respect. He is my new second-in-command."

Karai couldn't believe what she was hearing. "What? *I've* earned that job! Not some oversized cat in a scarf!"

"Enough!" Shredder growled. "Tiger Claw, take my daughter with you to capture Splinter and his Turtles. Karai, do not disobey him."

Karai said nothing. *I will prove to my father that I am more worthy of being his second-in-command than this hired employee!* she thought. Then she remembered what Leo had said to her on the rooftop—something about her real father. *But Shredder is my real father. Isn't he?*

CHAPTER 4

Under a starry sky, April O'Neil ran across the rooftops of New York City, vaulting over and clambering up walls. Casey Jones was close behind her, hurrying to keep up.

"So, April," he called to her, lifting his hockey mask onto the top of his head. "Vigilante-ing is cool and all, but how 'bout a *real* date?"

April turned to him, puzzled. "What do you call *this*?"

Casey slipped his arm around April's shoulder. "I was thinking, you know, something a little cozier. You, me—"

April started to smile. Then she heard a weird but familiar sound. "The Kraang!" she exclaimed.

"Nah," Casey said, shaking his head. "Aliens would just mess up my mix!"

Peering over the edge of the roof, April saw a long line of Kraang-droids marching into a glowing magenta triangle in the alley below. "There are so many of them," she whispered.

With his hockey sticks strapped to his back, Casey joined April. He watched the Kraang-droids march into the shining triangle. "So these are the robots you told me about?"

April nodded. "With the little brains inside, yeah. What are they *doing*?"

She lowered herself to a narrow ledge, and then jumped to the alley below, squatting behind a big metal trash bin. When she peeked around the corner of the bin, she saw that only a few more Kraang-droids were lined up to walk into the triangle. They were all disguised as black-haired New York businessmen, wearing black pin-striped suits and human masks.

"That's a new trick," she whispered.

Casey joined her behind the trash bin. "I got

this, Red," he said, lowering his hockey mask and pulling out a baseball bat. "Stay here."

He ran up behind the last droid in the line and smashed him with his bat. *WHAP!* The droid fell back, but it still punched Casey. April jumped into the fight, swinging her sharp-edged fan to slice the metal robot in half. A purple Kraang—a brainlike alien with eyes, a mouth, and six tentacles—flew out of the broken robot. It soared right at Casey . . .

. . . who WHACKED it! The alien fell to the ground, seeing stars.

The Kraang looked alarmed and scurried into the swirling triangle. It disappeared!

April walked up to the triangle. It seemed to be projected from a metal disk hovering in the air. When she touched the disk, the triangle disappeared, and the disk fell to the ground with a *CLANG!*

"Wow," she said, kneeling down to pick up the strange disk. "Let's take this to Donnie and let him check it out."

Casey frowned. He was pretty sure that mutant Turtle had a crush on April. And even though he was confident that April would prefer him to a mutated Turtle, he wasn't taking any chances. The less time April spent around Donnie, the better.

"Why not take it to a *real* laboratory?" he suggested, trying to keep the jealousy out of his voice so April wouldn't know why he didn't want to take the object to Donnie.

"Trust me," April scoffed, "Donnie's *way* ahead of most scientists!"

Leaving the broken robot lying in the alley, she led the way to the Turtles' secret lair down in the abandoned tunnels below the city. Casey had no choice but to follow her—there was no way he was going to leave April alone with Donnie.

CHAPTER 5

Once in Donnie's laboratory, April was excited to demonstrate the unusual Kraang object she found in the alley. All four Turtles had gathered in the lab for the demonstration. Donnie wasn't all that thrilled to see Casey, but he was always happy to see April.

"Then you press this button," April said, pressing the center of the strange disk, "and . . . portable portal!"

The glowing magenta triangle was projected from the device to the floor of the lab. Inside the triangle, the light pulsed and shifted. Patches of white and blue swirled around, too, though most of it remained magenta.

The Turtles stared at the triangle. They had never seen anything like it.

Donnie leaned forward to take a closer look. "Wow! The Kraang are always one step ahead!"

"How do you know it's a portal?" Leo asked.

"Simple," Casey said. "We saw those robot dudes walking into it. They didn't come out the other side. They just disappeared!"

Donnie put his hand to his chin, thinking. "I wonder if this Kraang device is what's behind the earthquakes. We're going to have to test it."

But Leo wasn't sure. He questioned whether testing an alien technology they knew nothing about was really wise—especially if the tech might have something to do with the recent earthquakes. "Think that's a good idea, Donnie?"

Donnie hesitated. On the one hand, he respected Leo's opinions and knew that caution was always smart. On the other hand, he was so intrigued by the mysterious portal that he couldn't wait to start analyzing it.

Waiting wasn't Casey's strong suit, either. "If you Turtles are going to be slow about it . . ."

"Slow? Turtles?" Raph said. "What's THAT supposed to mean?"

"It means," Casey said defiantly, "I'm going

through that portal! Right now!" He walked toward the glowing triangle, but Raph stopped him.

"You're crazy!" he said, poking Casey in the chest. "Nuts! Outta your gourd!" Using both hands, he shoved Casey, knocking him onto his butt. "I'M goin' first!" He turned, jumped right into the swirling light of the portal, and disappeared!

"Raph!" Leo shouted. But he was already gone.

There was no way Casey was going to miss out on this adventure. "Come on, Red!" he said, grabbing April's hand. He ran straight into the triangle, pulling April in with him.

"April!" Donnie cried. When he saw his secret crush disappear with Casey, Donnie didn't hesitate for a second. He refused to be left behind. "Wait for me!"

He jumped into the portal and disappeared.

Mikey and Leo were left standing there in the lab, staring at the magenta triangle. Leo wasn't sure what to do. He couldn't abandon his friends, but he had a bad feeling about just leaping through a Kraang portal. Who knew where they'd end up?

Mikey turned to Leo. For him, the decision was simple. "Can't let 'em go alone, dude!" Taking a deep breath and putting his hands together over his head as though he were diving into a swimming pool, he ran straight into the triangle and vanished. The portal rippled like a pond that had had a rock thrown into it.

"Mikey!" Leo called after his brother. He sighed and slapped his forehead. Then he ran into the glowing triangle himself.

For a moment, the empty lab was still. Then it started shaking. Another earthquake! The lights flickered, and chunks of cement fell from the ceiling. One chunk hit the Kraang device, knocking it to the floor. It slid into the wall, and the impact shut the device off. It stopped projecting the glowing magenta triangle.

The portal was closed!

CHAPTER 6

Leo jumped out of the portal and landed on . . . nothing. He took a few steps forward. It was as though he were walking on an invisible floor, high in the sky, with puffy white clouds floating below.

In front of him he saw two long rows of magenta triangles, stretching into the distance as far as he could see. He realized they were actually three-dimensional pyramids, not flat triangles.

The others stood in front of him, staring at the bizarre surroundings. "Okay," Raph said slowly. "This is . . . weird."

Mikey and April approached one of the magenta pyramids and looked through it. They saw an alien world, with shiny spheres hanging in the atmosphere.

"Wow," Donnie marveled. "It's like the Grand Central Station of dimensional travel!" He put his fist to his chin, thinking. "The Kraang must use it as a gateway between realities. . . ."

Behind Mikey, the magenta portal made an odd electronic sound and . . . disappeared! Mikey whipped around. When he saw what had happened, he grabbed his head and yelled, "Guys, the door's gone! We're trapped!"

"There are thousands of doors," Leo pointed out, trying to reassure everyone that they weren't trapped. "Everyone start searching for a way home!"

Donnie was amazed by the beauty of the alien world he saw through the first pyramid and wanted to share it with April. "Wow, look at this, April!"

She came over and looked into the pyramid Donnie was staring into. She saw an astonishing, snowy world. "Amazing," she gasped. "It's so beautiful. . . ." Donnie leaned his head closer to April's. . . .

But Casey saw what his rival was doing. "Check THIS out, Red!" he called. April left to join Casey in front of a different pyramid. Donnie scowled, and then walked over to see what Casey had found—a way back home?

But when the Turtles and April peered into the pyramid, they saw something very surprising. . . .

"It's US!" Mikey exclaimed. "But why do we look like dorks?"

The four Turtles, Casey, and April were all recognizable, but they looked like flat cartoon characters walking down the street together!

While Donnie, Raph, and Mikey stared at these bizarre cartoon versions of themselves, Leo moved on to another pyramid, searching for one that would take them back to their own world. But he found something very different. . . .

"Guys, look!" he called. "I think it's Dimension X!"

The others quickly joined him. *"Home of the Kraang,"* Raph hissed as he stared through the pyramid at the strange magenta world with spiked spheres and flying crafts buzzing through the sky.

"This place is makin' my brain melt!" Mikey

cried. April quickly covered his mouth with her hand and closed her eyes. "Shhh," she whispered. She was getting one of her psychic feelings. "I sense something . . . coming!"

As they stared into Dimension X, the Turtles were horrified to see a platform with two large Kraang-droids fly into view. But they didn't look like businessmen in suits. They looked like huge blue-green apes controlled by the Kraang sitting on top of them!

The droids growled and headed straight toward the pyramid portal!

"They're on to us!" Casey cried.

CHAPTER 7

A bolt of energy blasted out of the pyramid! The Turtles, Casey, and April ducked as it crackled over their heads. Two Kraang crafts came whizzing out of the portal!

Piloted by Kraang aliens, the small ships kept blasting magenta lightning bolts at the Turtles, who dove to dodge the zaps of energy.

"Biotroid, destroy!" commanded a robotic voice. Two of the blue-green ape-droids leaped out of the portal, swinging their gigantic fists. Mikey dodged the blows, and Donnie used his *bo* staff to knock the first ape-droid aside.

Wielding his two *katana* swords, Leo faced off against the other ape-droid. If only he could get a good, clear shot at the Kraang riding on top, sitting where a real ape's brain would be . . .

ZWIZZZZ! The ape-droid shot two sharp clip-on wires out of its chest, straight at Leo. He flipped, somersaulted, and twisted away from the droid, avoiding the deadly clips. But the ape-droid kept chasing him. . . .

"HYUNH!" Raph grunted as he vaulted onto the ape-droid's shoulders from behind. He slammed his *sais* down into the robot's shoulders, hoping to shut him down. But the ape-droid whirled around, punched Raph and sent him flying!

Casey saw one of the small Kraang ships flying toward him. "Casey Jones shoots . . . ," he said, calling his own moves like a sports announcer. He batted the ship away with his hockey stick. *WHACK!* The ship hurtled into one of the pyramids and disappeared. "He scores!"

The ape-droid that punched Raph held him down with his foot and drew back his fist, ready to deal Raph a punishing blow. But then . . . *CRACK!* April's sharp-edged fan smacked the droid in the head and spun right back into her hand! The ape-droid fell back, seeing stars.

But now it was mad—or maybe the Kraang controlling the droid was mad. It thumped its chest like an angry gorilla!

Leo flipped his way up onto the shoulders of the other ape-droid and plunged his swords into the device the Kraang was riding in, breaking it. The droid crashed to the ground, and the Kraang alien scrambled away on its tentacles.

The angry ape-droid who was beating its chest charged right at Mikey, Leo, and Raph!

"Here it comes!" Mikey yelled.

"LOOK OUT!" Raph warned.

The ape-droid launched itself through the air with both feet and both fists flying. *"YAAAU-UUUGH!"* screamed Leo, Raph, and Mikey as they were knocked into one of the magenta pyramids.

Donnie, Casey, and April ran up to the pyramid. "Guys! Let's follow 'em!" Donnie yelled. But a Kraang flew up in a tiny craft and hit a button on a remote control. The pyramid disappeared!

"They're gone!" April cried.

Knowing he was too high for them to reach, the Kraang taunted them, showing them the remote control.

"We gotta get that remote!" Casey said.

But the Kraang tossed the remote from one tentacle to another and into a different pyramid! The remote control was gone now, too!

Before Donnie, Casey, and April had any time to even think about this latest problem, another ape-droid dropped down in front of them. It turned around and its butt opened on a hinge, revealing the barrels of two big guns!

"Butt cannons!" Donnie said in disbelief. "RUN!"

The three friends turned and fled, dodging the blasts from the butt cannons.

CHAPTER 8

In a New York City alley, a cat dug through a garbage can. When it heard the humming sound of a large, glowing triangle that appeared several feet up in the air, it meowed and ran off.

Leo, Raph, and Mikey fell out of the portal right into the garbage bin. "WHOOOAAA!"

Mikey popped up out of the garbage container with a lampshade on his head. "Whoa, guys," he said, trying to see through the lampshade. "What dimension are we in?"

Raph knocked the lampshade off Mikey's head. Leo vaulted out of the garbage container and stared up into the starry night sky. "The others are trapped over there," he said.

"Yeah," agreed Raph, climbing out of the bin. "And the *smart* member of the team is trapped with 'em!" Mikey glared at Raph, figuring the insult was aimed at him, and grunted. He followed Raph out of the garbage container.

Raph confronted Leo. "This is *your* fault, Leo! If you hadn't gotten us— Whoaaa!"

The ground was vibrating again, throwing them off-balance. When the shaking stopped, Leo said, "We gotta find the source of these quakes!" The three Turtles ran off down the alley.

Tiger Claw loomed above them on a nearby roof and watched them go. He turned to Karai, who was kneeling at the base of a water tower. "You have your instructions," he growled to her. She nodded. She still didn't like taking orders from Tiger Claw, but she had to obey Shredder.

The three Turtles were still running farther down the block when suddenly, Tiger Claw jumped in front of them and blocked their way. "Who the heck is *that*?" Raph asked, stopping in his tracks.

The assassin drew himself up to his full height, towering over the teenagers. "You may call me . . . TIGER CLAW!" he roared.

"I knew it!" Mikey said. "I was *totally* going to name him Tiger Claw!"

Tiger Claw pulled one of his blasters out of its holster, spun it in his hand, and aimed its big, triangular barrel right at the Turtles. A red glow shone from inside the barrel as the weapon powered up. "I ask only once," he snarled. "Summon your rat master!"

"Sorry, pal," Raph said as he drew out his *sais* and advanced on the huge mutant. "I'm not a cat person!"

The sentence was barely out of Raph's mouth before Tiger Claw fired. The Turtles leaped out of the way as the heat blast hit the pavement. Raph dodged another burst by flipping off a garage door, but then he fell to the ground.

"Raph!" Leo yelled. He ran straight toward Tiger Claw, whipping his *katana* blades out of their sheaths. He swung the swords, but Tiger

Claw ducked, leaped over Leo, and hit him with a blast.

Mikey twirled his *nunchucks.* Tiger Claw aimed both of his blasters at him, stopping him cold. "You are nothing but cubs," the assassin said, growling.

"Heh, heh," Mikey said. "Nice kitty! Lemme see if I have some catnip on me. . . ."

Tiger Claw's growl became a roar! He fired his other blaster. Mikey jumped out of the way just as a cluster of sharp crystals formed where he'd been standing. While the red blaster shot heat, the blue blaster seemed to be shooting intense cold.

Mikey jumped up onto a fire escape and started to climb. "C'mon, bros!" he called. "We gotta get to high ground!"

Leo and Raph got up and followed him as Tiger Claw blasted the side of the building they were climbing. Then he fired up the jetpack on his back and zoomed up after them!

Back in the inter-dimensional space, Donnie, Casey, and April were running down the corridor of magenta pyramids, trying to escape from the ape-droid. Suddenly, it vaulted over them. The ape-droid was in the perfect position to fire his butt cannons again!

"I got this!" Casey said, hitting the ape-droid with his hockey stick. The droid pitched forward, and his head went into one of the pyramids.

Donnie and April ran up behind the droid, pushed as hard as they could, and managed to shove the massive robot through the portal!

"That was too close," April said.

Casey immediately challenged Donnie. "All

right, Donnie—how do we get outta here? You're the 'expert,' gap-tooth!"

Donnie and Casey got nose to nose, glaring into each other's eyes. "'Gap-tooth'?" Donnie said. "Look in the mirror lately, cave mouth?"

April was looking through another pyramid. "Guys, stop!" she said. "Check this out!"

Casey and Donnie hurried over and stared into the pyramid she was pointing to. "Wow," Donnie said. "Looks like another part of Dimension X!"

Inside that dimension, Kraang-droids were using some kind of energy prods to move a huge worm creature through a portal.

Casey thought the worm looked incredibly disgusting. "Ew! What is *that*?" he said loudly.

Unfortunately, the Kraang-droids heard him.

They turned and stared at Casey, April, and Donnie. One of them said in a robotic voice, "Kraang is aware of spies in that doorway where Kraang is not, but soon will be!"

"I think we're in serious trouble," April said.

Suddenly, they were surrounded by six

Kraang-droids, whose weapons were aimed right at them.

All three raised their hands slowly. "For the record," Casey said defiantly, "I don't count this as a surrender!"

CHAPTER 10

Back in New York City, Leo, Mikey, and Raph reached higher ground—the rooftop of a multistory building.

It didn't do them much good, though.

Tiger Claw jetted up to the roof and started firing his blasters the second he touched down. He shot his red heat blaster first. As Raph flew past him, he dodged the *sais* attack and switched to his blue cold blaster to fire another round.

Holding his *katana* swords, Leo launched himself at Tiger Claw, who ducked, fired a blue blast, and twirled his blaster around his finger.

The Turtles may have outnumbered him three to one, but Tiger Claw's skill in martial arts exceeded their own. He was just too experienced for them to defeat.

But they weren't giving up. No way.

Spinning his *nunchucks,* Mikey launched himself at Tiger Claw just as he was catching one of his blasters behind his back. The huge mutant whirled around and fired another blast of cold in Mikey's direction.

Then Tiger Claw aimed both of his weapons at Leo and alternated red and blue blasts as Leo somersaulted away from him. Sharp clusters of cold crystals formed where the blue blasts hit.

The Turtles fought their tough opponent the way their sensei taught them, taking turns drawing his fire while the others tried to attack. They kept watching for some weakness on Tiger Claw's part, waiting for him to make a mistake.

And waiting, and waiting . . .

Suddenly, Tiger Claw fired up his jetpack.

He fired both weapons as he rose into the night air above the roof, knocking Mikey to the ground. "Mikey!" Leo called to his brother.

Raph grew enraged. It was okay for *him* to mess with Mikey, but someone else? No! When Tiger Claw zoomed back down to the roof, Raph ran straight at him, swinging his *sais*. For a moment, it looked as though Raph, through sheer anger, was gaining the advantage over Tiger Claw.

But the wily assassin had more tricks up his sleeve. He used his jetpack to blast *away* from Raph and loaded his weapon with a special cartridge. He took aim at Raph and fired. . . .

A spinning rope sliced through the air and wrapped around Raph! He fell to the ground, bound by the rope, helpless. He struggled to get free, but the rope was too tight.

Tiger Claw flew over to Mikey, who was still lying on the ground in a daze. Tiger Claw lifted him by one foot and held him upside-down over an open chimney. Sparks flew up into the night air. Mikey groaned.

"You are defeated!" Tiger Claw growled. "Summon your master, or the little one goes into the furnace!"

Even though he was upside-down, Mikey held up his hands with his palms facing out, making a STOP gesture. "Don't do it, Leo!" he cried.

Still holding one of his *katana* swords in front of him, Leo glared at Tiger Claw.

Behind him, bundled facedown on the ground, Raph warned, "It's a trap for Splinter!"

"Of course it's a trap!" Leo answered. "But tell me the part where I have a choice!"

Far below the city, in the Turtles' secret lair, Splinter sat with his legs crossed and his hands balanced on his knees, meditating. Next to him, under a glass dome, sat a phone shaped like a wheel of yellow cheese.

It rang. *BRINNNNG! BRINNNNG!*

Splinter opened his eyes, startled. "The cheese phone!" he said. "Truly, an emergency!"

He hurried to the phone, lifting the glass dome and picking up the handset to the old-fashioned corded phone. *"Moshi moshi,"* he said, a Japanese greeting. He listened to the voice on the other end and said, "Leonardo! What is the problem?" He listened some more and looked grim. "Do not fear, my son," Splinter said. "I am on my way!"

CHAPTER
11

Tiger Claw tied the three brothers together, back-to-back, on the roof. No matter how much they struggled against the rope, they couldn't get loose. They were sitting by the broken chimney that led down to the fiery furnace. The assassin was watching them carefully, waiting for their master to arrive to save them.

"I can't believe you called him," Raph said to Leo angrily. "If anything happens to Splinter—"

"What else could I do, Raph?" Leo asked, exasperated.

"The rat!" Tiger Claw demanded impatiently. "Where is he?"

The three Turtles stared at Tiger Claw and

then looked away. They weren't going to tell him anything.

Tiger Claw scowled, his whiskers quivering with anger. "One push, and you ALL go into the furnace!" he threatened.

Raph defiantly looked the mutant in the eye. "Just wait, Tiger Claw," he said. "Splinter is gonna kick that little stub of a tail so deep in your striped—"

"SILENCE!" Tiger Claw roared. "I'm tired of waiting! Your lives end *now*!" He put his foot against the three brothers and started pushing them toward the broken chimney.

"This is it!" Mikey cried. "I love you, guys! Raph, it was me who ate your last piece of chocolate pepperoni pizza! I'm sorry, man! I was SO HUNGRY!"

Just as the Turtles were about to fall into the furnace, a clear, strong voice rang out from above. "Release my sons . . . NOW!"

Tiger Claw looked up and saw Splinter on a higher roof. He was holding a staff, standing in front of a bright full moon.

Speaking in Japanese, Tiger Claw said, "An ancient proverb says, 'Even a cornered rat will bite a cat.' Is that so?"

Splinter smiled. "Hmph!" he answered. Then in Japanese, "Come find out."

In one rapid move, Tiger Claw reached behind him, grabbed a powerful blaster, and fired it at Splinter five times. *BLAM! BLAM! BLAM! BLAM! BLAM!*

Leaping from ledge to ledge, Splinter dodged the blasts, keeping in constant motion. He almost jumped right onto Tiger Claw, but the huge mutant stepped back just in time. The assassin kept blasting his weapon, but Splinter kept evading his shots, even swatting bricks at Tiger Claw with his staff as he spun across the damaged roof. Three of the bricks hit Tiger Claw in the face, knocking him head over heels!

Growling, Tiger Claw pulled out a sword with a broad, sharp blade. He spun the sword, glaring at Splinter. "Bah!" he said, done with his blaster for the moment. "I prefer to slice you into bite-sized pieces!"

Roaring, Tiger Claw leaped forward, pointing the deadly tip of his sword right at Splinter. The rat didn't hesitate. He leaped forward to meet his enemy, and their weapons clashed in midair!

Led by the Kraang-droids, April, Donnie, and Casey walked out of the magenta pyramid and looked around. They were in an empty New York City subway tunnel!

In his robotic, metallic voice, one of the Kraang-droids ordered, "You will continue marching from the place you are to the place you are not yet!"

The prisoners spoke quietly among themselves. "Seems like the Kraang still need to do a little work on their droids' language software," April observed.

"At least we're back in New York," Donnie said.

"Didn't they mention feeding us something?" Casey asked. "I'm hungry."

April shook her head. "No, they said they'd feed us TO something. Something called a . . ." She tried to remember the long, complicated name.

"A Kraathatrogon," Donnie said, happy to know the answer. "Which is . . . Actually, I have no clue what it is."

They walked down the empty subway tunnel in silence.

But Casey was done being ordered around by a bunch of alien robots. "We can wait around to be eaten," he said quietly, "OR WE CAN MAKE A MOVE!"

He flipped his glove, releasing a bent metal device from his sleeve. Attached to a battery, it glowed blue with electric energy. Casey whipped around and pressed the device against the metal robot. Blue energy crackled all over the droid's body!

Since Casey had started the fight, April and Donnie didn't have much choice but to join in. April threw her sharp fan right at the chest of another Kraang-droid and sent him flying. Donnie whipped a throwing star at a steam valve, releasing clouds of white steam into the subway tunnel to hide their escape.

"Let's go!" Donnie shouted. As they ran through the tunnel, the remaining Kraang-droid fired blasts of magenta energy at them.

April noticed a side tunnel with a door in it. She skidded to a stop, and the two boys ran right past her. "This way!" she called after them as she headed toward the door. Donnie and Casey turned around and followed her into the side tunnel.

They kicked the old metal door open and sprinted through it as magenta blasts burst all around them. "Go! Move!" Casey yelled. He grabbed the door, slammed it shut, and shoved his old baseball bat through two brackets to hold the door closed.

They escaped from the Kraang-droids. Now they could stop running and figure out where they were.

"Wow!" Donnie exclaimed when he realized what they were walking through. "The old pneumatic subway tunnels! Built in the 1800s—nobody uses 'em now!"

As they kept walking, April heard something. "What's that gross slobbering sound?"

Donnie listened for a moment. "It sounds worse than Mikey eating pizza!" He hurried forward to find the source of the sickening sound. Casey and April rushed to follow him.

They reached the end of the old tunnel, where it opened out into a huge underground chamber, lit by an eerie green light. In the center of the chamber was a gigantic piece of Kraang technology, with pipes and hoses leading to . . .

. . . four enormous, segmented white worms!

CHAPTER 13

Donnie, April, and Casey crawled to the very edge of the tunnel to get a closer look. "Those must be the Kraathatrogons!" Donnie whispered. There was nothing like them on Earth.

"The Kraatha . . . Krothag . . . Kraathag . . .," Casey whispered, trying to pronounce the long, unfamiliar word. Then he just gave up. "'Space worms' is easier to say," he decided, grinning at April.

But April frowned, studying the gigantic worms. These alien creatures gave her a bad feeling. . . .

"*RUUAAAHH!*" roared one of the worms, rising up and sending two of its Kraang-droid handlers flying. It slammed its massive body back on the ground. *WHAM!* The whole chamber shook, and pieces of concrete fell from the ceiling.

Casey, April, and Donnie fell back, dodging the falling pieces. "Whoa!"

"It's the worms!" Donnie suddenly realized.

"Duh," Casey said. "Obviously it's the worms. We just saw one rear up like a crazy stallion and slam its body down onto the ground. How could we have missed that?"

Donnie gritted his teeth. "Those worms are what's been causing all the earthquakes in New York!"

A Kraang-droid dragged the Kraathatrogon by a metal chain, forcing it back into its place. Another Kraang-droid carried a long hose with a huge black nozzle attachment toward the worm.

"But . . . why?" Casey asked. "Why would the Kraang bring their giant space worms through a portal into the old subway tunnels?"

"Look!" April whispered. She pointed at the Kraang-droid with the nozzle. He was attaching it to the side of the worm! "They're milking the worms for . . . mutagen?"

Sure enough, some kind of liquid began to pump out of the worm, flowing through the hose and up into a glowing green storage tank.

"By Darwin's beard!" Donnie exclaimed. "THIS is where the mutagen comes from!"

"Mutagen?" Casey asked.

"That's the stuff the Kraang use to mutate creatures—kind of a green ooze," April explained. She caught herself then, hoping talk of mutation wouldn't hurt Donnie's feelings.

But he didn't look at all offended. He looked amazed. "Fascinating," he said. "And . . ."

". . . disgusting!" April said. Then she felt someone touch her. Casey was right next to her, so she glared at him and said, "Stop that!"

Casey looked confused. "Stop what?"

April ignored him, but then felt something again. She wheeled on Casey. "I'm serious! I said stop!" Casey held up both hands, protesting his innocence.

April looked down and saw . . .

. . . a small white worm nuzzling her leg! Well, small compared to the giant worms. Compared to an earthworm, it was huge! *"Yah!"* April shrieked.

"AAUUUGH!" Casey yelled.

Casey stepped back and bonked the worm on the head with his hockey stick. It immediately opened its mouth wide, showing three jaws bristling with razor-sharp teeth! It hissed angrily, giving them away!

One of the Kraang-droids spoke to the other droids. "We have been discovered in the place that was meant to be undiscovered!"

"UNLEASH THE KRAATHATROGON!" ordered another.

The nozzles on the side of the worm released and dropped to the floor. Untethered, the

Kraathatrogon quickly found the tunnel Donnie, April, and Casey were hiding in. It reared back, opened its huge mouth, and roared!

The three friends flinched and looked up in wonder. "I don't think I have a big enough hockey stick for that thing," Casey said shakily.

"I'm in charge while my father is in Japan,"
says Karai.

The Turtles battle Karai's ninjas—and the
vicious Rahzar!

Donatello is tracking a series of strange earthquakes around New York City.

Shredder returns from Japan with a villain named Tiger Claw.

Raphael is ready to enter a Kraang portal
to Dimension X.

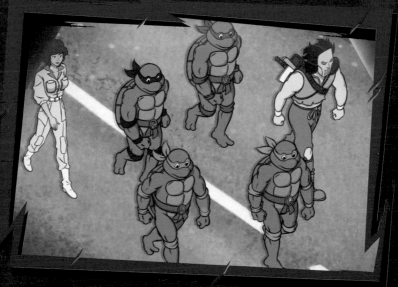

The Turtles see themselves
in another dimension.

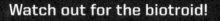

Watch out for the biotroid!

The Kraang control giant worms from
Dimension X called Kraathatrogons.

The Kraang are on guard.

Leonardo, Raphael, and Michelangelo
are captured by Tiger Claw!

Splinter battles Tiger Claw!

A Kraathatrogon is loose beneath
New York City!

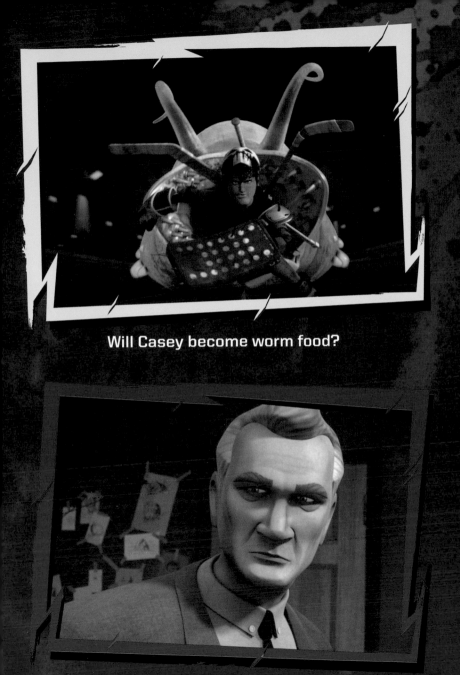

Will Casey become worm food?

Journalist Jack Kurtzman has figured out the Kraang's plan—but is it too late?

April and Casey hold on for a worm ride!

Showdown with a villain!

CHAPTER 14

On the rooftop, Tiger Claw roared, lunging at Splinter with his wide, cruel sword. Splinter parried with his staff and slipped around the massive tiger-man. The three Turtles, bound together near the smoking chimney, watched the incredible display of fighting skills.

Splinter blocked every one of Tiger Claw's sword strokes, all the while landing three punishing blows of his staff on Tiger Claw's face, knocking him back.

"You'll pay for that, rodent!" Tiger Claw snarled. He swiftly raised his sword and brought it crashing down on Splinter's staff.

The staff broke! Splinter was left holding half a staff in each hand.

Tiger Claw laughed—an evil, gloating laugh. "Now you are defenseless!"

"A ninja is never defenseless," Splinter said. He held his hand up, and three metal throwing blades appeared along his fingers. Flicking his wrist, he hurled them straight at Tiger Claw.

The mutant's eyes widened with alarm. He drew back his sword to knock the whizzing blades of steel away, but one caught his shoulder. He felt the searing pain.

Tiger Claw flew at Splinter with his sword. As the two fought back and forth across the roof, the three Turtles cheered their master on.

"You got him, Sensei!" Mikey shouted, craning his neck to see all the action.

"Slap the stripes off that cat!" Raph added. It was killing him to have to sit and watch, instead of jumping in to help his father.

Splinter somersaulted, slipping right under Tiger Claw's blade. He popped up under the mutant's thick striped arm, grabbed it with one hand, and chopped it with the other, so that . . .

. . . Tiger Claw dropped his sword right into Splinter's hand! He immediately whacked Tiger Claw sending him skidding across the roof.

But the assassin was well trained. Raising himself up on one knee, he pulled out his blaster, aimed it at Splinter, and fired. A spinning rope flew through the air at the mutant rat.

"You will not trip me up so easily!" Splinter declared, his eyes narrowing. He focused all his attention on the rope flying straight toward him. At the last possible second, he sprang into the air, reached down, and snagged the rope!

Landing on his feet, he spun the rope in his hand and flung it back at Tiger Claw. The tiger-man ducked the rope but made the mistake of turning his head to watch the rope go by. That was when Splinter attacked.

First, he used Tiger Claw's sword to knock the blaster out of his hand. Then he came right at Tiger Claw, swinging his sword to put the mutant off-balance. As Tiger Claw helplessly backed away from Splinter, the rat kept chopping the tiger-man in the face and chest, delivering a series of painful blows. *WHAM! WHAP! CHOP! BAM!*

Finally, Tiger Claw was teetering on the edge of the roof. Gasping, he glanced down at the street far below. When he looked back, he saw the point of his own sword inches from his face.

Splinter spoke calmly. "We shall see if a cat always lands on its feet."

"NOW!" Tiger Claw yelled.

On a nearby roof, Karai stood underneath a huge billboard advertising pest control. Taking careful aim, she shot her weapon. A dart zipped through the air, heading straight for Splinter!

ZZZZWIP! The dart struck Splinter's neck, sticking there. "Hm?" he said, pulling the small dart out of his skin and examining it.

The drugged dart did its work quickly. Splinter staggered back, dropping Tiger Claw's sword and collapsing to his hands and knees. The world seemed to be spinning around him.

"Ha!" Tiger Claw laughed, rubbing his wounded arm. "You lose, rat!"

Splinter looked up and saw Karai striding across the roof toward him. Staring coldly, she tossed her dart gun aside. She stopped a few feet from Splinter and smiled a small, satisfied smile. She knew she'd carried out her orders perfectly.

Splinter looked up at Karai helplessly. He stretched his hand out to her, cried "Miwa!" and collapsed, passing out.

Karai's eyes widened as she stared at her victim.

"Karai!" Leo called to the *kunoichi*.

Karai's eyes darted toward Leo.

"Karai, please don't do this," Leo pleaded. "Splinter . . . he's your father! Your *true* father!"

Her eyes narrowed. "Liar!" she called out. "You'd say *anything* to save him!"

"No! I swear it!" Leo insisted. "He's your father! Hamato Yoshi!" He spoke the name given to the man who had mutated into the rat, Splinter.

Karai looked confused, then angry. "If you won't be silent," she warned, raising her sword above her head, "I'll silence you!"

CHAPTER 15

The three Turtles gasped!

But as Karai's sword came slicing down through the night air, it was blocked by another sword. *CLANG!*

Tiger Claw had blocked Karai's blow!

"What?" Karai asked, dumbfounded that Tiger Claw had dared to stop her deadly attack.

Tiger Claw pushed Karai's sword away. "Master Shredder desires them alive. He wants the pleasure of finishing the Turtles *himself.*"

Karai sheathed her sword. "Fine," she reluctantly agreed. "Let's deal with the rat first." She and Tiger Claw strode back to Splinter.

Tiger Claw did *not* sheathe his sword.

"Leave him alone, Karai!" Raph snarled, struggling against the ropes. "Or you're gonna answer to *me*!"

"My sons," Splinter managed to gasp. "Go . . . NOW!"

Summoning all his strength and skill, Splinter whipped three sharp throwing stars across the roof toward his sons. They neatly sliced the ropes that bound them, freeing the astonished Turtles.

"RUN!" Splinter yelled.

Tiger Claw ran over to Splinter and savagely kicked him in the chest, sending him sprawling. He fell off the roof, landing on a ledge a few feet below.

"SPLINTER!" Leo cried out, reaching toward him. He wanted to run to his sensei, but Raph grabbed his brother's arm.

"We gotta come back for him, Leo—MOVE!"

As Tiger Claw fired his heat blaster, the three Turtles dashed off the roof, leaping across to the fire escape on the next building.

"Don't let them escape!" Karai ordered,

forgetting that she wasn't in charge anymore.

But it was an order Tiger Claw didn't need to hear. He was already leaping across to the fire escape in pursuit of the Turtles.

Mikey pulled out one of his smoke bombs and hurled it down onto the floor of the fire escape. *FWOOM!* A cloud of purple smoke filled the fire escape.

When the smoke cleared, Tiger Claw was alone. The Turtles had disappeared! He stood up and growled.

Back on the nearby roof, Karai turned her back on Tiger Claw, facing Splinter. "At least we still have the rat," she snarled.

Splinter lay on the ledge, out cold.

CHAPTER 16

Pedestrians strolled past a mailbox on a New York City sidewalk. Suddenly, the earth jolted. They stopped, startled. What was causing all these small earthquakes?

The cause was far below them. Deep in the old abandoned subway tunnels beneath the streets, Donnie, April, and Casey ran for their lives. The huge Kraathatrogon was chasing them, lifting its long body and slamming it down on the old subway tracks.

"Run!" Donnie yelled, trying to be heard above the pounding sounds of the moving worm. "FASTER!"

The worm was gaining on them. The three

friends were too busy looking over their shoulders at the beast to notice a gap in the subway track. They all tripped and fell—"*YAAAAAHH!*"—landing facedown in a small space a couple of feet below the surface they had been running on. The worm was on them . . .

. . . and then passed right over them! It was like being underneath a rushing freight train!

Donnie, April, and Casey looked at each other. Were they safe? They cautiously peered up over the edge of the hole they had fallen into, only to see . . .

. . . the small worm that had nuzzled up against April's leg just moments ago! Where had it come from? Startled, Donnie slapped the small worm and ran. The worm didn't seem to mind. April and Casey followed the sprinting Turtle.

But so did the huge Kraathatrogon! When it felt the vibrations of its prey running in the opposite direction, it turned its bulky body around and scooted back the way it had come.

April was getting exhausted. "We gotta slow it down," she gasped.

Casey responded instantly. "I'm on it!" he cried, releasing the skating wheels on his gym shoes.

April and Donnie looked over their shoulders, watching Casey skate toward the rushing worm. "Casey, no!" April yelled.

But Casey kept on skating toward the Kraathatrogon. He pulled out a can of yellow spray paint and shook it up. When he was a few feet from the worm, he hurled the can into the monster's gaping mouth.

The can exploded inside the worm's mouth, spraying yellow paint over its teeth and chin. A yellow cloud rose from its mouth as it reared back and then fell onto the track.

Casey skated up to the fallen creature. "YES!" he shouted, thrilled that his paint-can maneuver had succeeded.

Or had it?

The worm lifted its head just as quickly as it fell, opened its huge mouth, and roared at Casey.

"NOOOOO!" Casey screamed, turning and skating away. The worm chased after him, not slowed a bit by the paint can now rattling deep inside its belly.

April looked back and urged him on. "Casey! HURRY!"

He skated as fast as he could, but the worm was getting closer.

Donnie spotted a ladder leading out of the tunnel. He jumped, snagging one of the rungs. Right away, he whipped around and extended his *bo* staff toward April.

April flung herself toward the staff, grabbing it with her right hand. Donnie hauled her onto the ladder.

Hanging onto a rung of the ladder, Donnie extended his *bo* staff as far as he could, holding it out toward the subway tracks. "JONES!" he yelled above the roar of the rushing worm. "The staff!"

Casey forced his legs to push harder. He launched himself toward the staff with his arms outstretched . . .

. . . but the giant worm heaved forward and swallowed him!

"NOOO!" April screamed.

"CASEY!" Donnie shouted.

Donnie and April could only watch, stunned, as the worm rushed on down the subway tunnel, turned around a bend, and disappeared.

"He's . . . gone." April choked out the words. "He's gone." She closed her eyes and laid her head against Donnie's shell. He put his arm on her back and drew her close.

"I'm so sorry, April," Donnie said sincerely. "I truly am."

April shut her eyes tighter, trying to forget the sight of the Kraathatrogon engulfing Casey Jones.

CHAPTER 17

Back in the Teenage Mutant Ninja Turtles' secret lair, Leo was tightly wrapping a bandage around Mikey's green arm. "Ow, ow, ow, ow, . . . OWWW!" Mikey cried. Leo ignored his brother's complaining and kept bandaging his arm.

Mikey wasn't the only brother with complaints. "This is YOUR fault, Leo!" Raph insisted, tossing down the ice pack he'd been holding to his head and pointing an accusing finger at Leo. "If you hadn't called Splinter, we wouldn't be in this mess!"

Leo answered his brother's accusation patiently. "I didn't have a choice, Raph. It was him or Mikey. I thought . . . I thought Sensei would take care of himself." Leo looked away. He felt just as bad about what had happened to Splinter as Raph did.

But Leo's answer did nothing to calm Raph's anger. He crossed his arms and said, "Well, ya thought wrong!"

Leo stood up, trying to look as commanding as possible. "We know where they took him," he said, facing Raph. "Shredder's lair! We do this for Splinter!"

Mikey thrust a finger into the air. "There comes a time, brothers, when history is forged like . . ."

He paused, trying to think of something history could be forged like.

". . . melted cheese!" He pressed his hands together. "It sticks together, as ONE!" He worked his hands as though he were squeezing a lump of melted cheese. "But it's still soft and squishy in the middle!"

Mikey licked his lips and closed his eyes, thinking about the hot melted cheese on a delicious pizza. He could really go for one from Antonio's right now. . . .

He opened his eyes, again aware that he was giving his brothers an inspirational speech about going on a dangerous mission, only to see them staring at him. He decided to wrap it up, and raised a defiant fist in the air. "ARE YOU WITH ME?"

Raph just shook his head. "Lamest. Speech. Ever," he said. "But . . . I'm with you."

The three brothers put their hands in, pressing one on top of the other. "Let's do this!" Leo said.

They started preparing right away.

Raph put thick metal bands around his hands with jagged claws extending from them.

Leo carefully coiled a rope with grappling hooks on the end.

And Mikey got out his trusty old box of fireworks. He opened it, gazed at the explosives, smoke bombs, and bottle rockets, and chuckled to himself slyly. This mission to rescue Splinter was dangerous, but Mikey saw no reason why it couldn't also be fun. . . .

CHAPTER 18

Donnie and April climbed the metal rungs of the subway ladder up the wall until they were right underneath a round manhole cover. They were still shocked by what had happened to Casey. Donnie lifted the heavy steel cover and climbed up onto the street. He looked around and saw no one.

"Okay, coast is clear," he told April. He helped her climb out of the manhole.

She was clearly upset. "This is so terrible," she cried. "Poor Casey!" Then she got a determined look on her face and placed her hands on Donnie's shoulders. "We have to find a way to stop those space worms once and for—"

But before she could finish her sentence, the

ground started to shake! "WHOA! WHAA!" she and Donnie yelled as they lurched backward and forward, falling to the ground. Trash cans and debris rolled by.

When the shaking stopped, Donnie got to his feet and helped April up. "You're right about stopping those worms!" he said. "And we know one man who knows more about the Kraang than anyone!"

Donnie and April were soon perched on a fire escape outside an apartment window. Sirens blared in the distance. Donnie kept a lookout as April knelt by the window and gently rapped on the glass with her knuckles. No one opened the window. April looked up at Donnie and shook her head.

She stood and looked in the window, leaning against the glass. Donnie joined her. Suddenly, a light snapped on, shining right in their eyes!

When their eyes adjusted, they could see who

was shining the light from inside the apartment—
Jack Kurtzman, the man they had come to see. The
rest of the apartment was dark as the man with gray
hair, thick eyebrows, and large, intelligent blue eyes
held the powerful source of illumination.

When he realized who was outside his window, he lowered the flashlight. "Great Caesar's
Ghost!" he said. "Quick! Get in before you're
spotted!"

He unlocked the bolt and raised the window.
April and Donnie climbed through and stepped
into the dingy apartment. The gray walls were
covered with photos and newspaper articles con-
nected by strings and thumbtacks, and the furni-
ture was old and worn.

Kurtzman shut the window and looked out to
see if anyone had seen Donnie and April come in.
Then he turned and faced them, looking concerned.
"This is about the earthquake situation, isn't it?"

As he crossed to a bulletin board on the wall,
April said, "You're never going to guess what's
causing it, Mr. Kurtzman."

He snatched four black-and-white photos off the bulletin board and examined them for a moment. "Call me Jack," Kurtzman said, tossing the photos down on a table. April and Donnie leaned in to look. She gasped. They were pictures of the Kraathatrogons in the subway tunnels!

It was clear that Jack Kurtzman was well aware of what was causing all the earthquakes.

He stared at the photos. "I named the Kraang's little scheme 'The Manhattan Project.'"

CHAPTER 19

Splinter groaned and slowly opened his eyes. He felt terrible. Where was he?

As his vision came back into focus, he saw Tiger Claw standing over him with a bucket of water. "Wake up, little rat!" he snarled as he threw the cold water in Splinter's face.

Tiger Claw tossed the metal bucket aside. Fishface came into Splinter's view to join Tiger Claw and stare down at him. The purple mutant grinned, showing his jagged teeth. "Nice work, Tiger Claw!" he said fawningly. "You finally captured the great Splinter!"

Splinter tried to move his arms, but they were chained behind his back. He was lying facedown on cold stone. He realized where he was: Shredder's lair.

Rahzar stood next to Fishface and Tiger Claw. The three made a nice, bizarre trio of mutants. They were watching Splinter carefully.

"So, is the poison going to finish him or what?" Rahzar asked in his gravelly voice.

Poison, Splinter remembered. *From the dart in my neck. The one shot by . . . Miwa. My own daughter shot me with poison.*

Tiger Claw frowned. "Most men would have expired by now, but it's only weakened him. He may be small, but he's tough as iron."

Shredder marched into the chamber followed by Karai. If the leader of the Foot Clan was happy to have captured his greatest enemy, he didn't show it. As he approached Rahzar and Fishface, he dismissed them, using the names they went by before their transformation into mutants. "Bradford, Xever . . . leave us." They bowed obediently and slinked out.

Splinter managed to rise to his knees. Tiger Claw towered over him with his arms folded across his chest, keeping a watchful eye on the ninja.

Shredder came to a stop right in front of Splinter. "Hamato Yoshi," he said in his deep voice, sounding highly satisfied. "So you have come to this: a wretched rat-man waiting to be put out of his misery."

Splinter showed no fear, even though he still felt sick from the poison. "At least I do not wear a mask, hiding what little humanity I have left."

"It is because of YOU that I wear this mask!" Shredder snarled, remembering the long-ago battle and fire in Japan.

Splinter shook his head sadly. "All these years," he said. "You continue to deceive yourself . . . and everyone around you." As he said this last part, he looked directly at Karai. She looked surprised, and then remembered what Leo told her about her real father.

Shredder was enraged by Splinter's last remark. "You DARE?" he said. Long, lethal blades shot out of the armor he wore over his hands. He raised one hand high above his head. "NOW IT ENDS!" he bellowed.

Splinter prepared himself to die.

But as Shredder roared in triumph and sliced the razor-sharp blades through the air toward Splinter's exposed neck, Karai flung out her hand and cried, "No, Father!"

Shredder stopped his hand fractions of an inch from Splinter's neck. He glared at Karai, shocked. "*You* would stop me?"

Karai looked Shredder in the eye, holding his angry gaze. "You'd kill your greatest enemy while he's poisoned and chained?

What about honor? *Everything you've taught me!*"

Tiger Claw stood next to Karai with his powerful arms crossed over his chest. "The girl is right, Master Shredder."

"Hmph," Shredder grunted, retracting his blades into his armor. He turned his back and started walking toward the door. "Very well. Gather the Foot. I will offer Hamato Yoshi one last fight." He left, with Tiger Claw behind him.

As Karai passed Splinter, he asked her, "Why did you help me?"

She paused, staring straight ahead. "I don't know." Then she shot him a scornful glance. "Maybe because you looked so pathetic!"

She started to walk out, but Splinter had something more to say to her, though it still pained him to speak. "You have your mother's spirit," he said in a low voice. "So fierce, and yet . . . so scared."

Karai wheeled around. Anger flashed in her eyes. "Never speak of my mother again!" She hung her head and closed her eyes. "You ruined my family! *You ruined all our lives!*"

She strode angrily out of the chamber.

In a soft voice full of pain, Splinter said, "No. It was . . . Oroku Saki." He repeated Shredder's Japanese name. *"Oroku . . . Saki . . ."*

He collapsed to the floor.

Back in Jack Kurtzman's apartment, April was looking at a copy of *Weekly Weird News*. The headline on the cover screamed, "BAT FREAK FOUND IN TUNNEL!" Kurtzman seemed interested in every odd thing that came his way—including mutant Turtles and giant space worms.

Donnie was sitting on Kurtzman's ugly green couch, pumping him for more information about the Kraathatrogon. Jack seemed eager to share. "So, these worms are only children?" Donnie asked. "How big are the adults?"

"Huge!" Kurtzman answered, spreading a well-worn diagram across his stained coffee table. It was covered with drawings of the worms and notes about their size and habits. He set a salt-shaker on the paper to keep it from rolling up like a scroll. "Some are hundreds of feet long! The Kraang have been importing the worms from Dimension X to suck out their mutagen. It's kinda like milking a cow. . . ."

He demonstrated by using his hands to pretend he was milking a cow.

April was grossed out. "Okay, okay, we get it. Thanks. How do we stop them?"

Kurtzman shrugged. "No clue how to stop 'em. But I know the Kraang ride these puppies." He pointed to a drawing on his diagram. "You see these antennae on its head? The Kraang grab 'em and pull on 'em to steer the worms, like using the reins on a horse." He picked up the saltshaker and moved it over the drawing like a worm. Salt spilled onto the paper.

"Why didn't I think of it before?" Donnie exclaimed. "Salt!"

April looked confused. "Salt? What do you—" Her cell phone rang in her back pocket.

She pulled it out, saying "Hold on a second. . . ."

When she looked at her phone's screen to see who was calling, she saw a picture of . . . CASEY! She stood up, amazed. "It's CASEY!" She answered the phone. "Casey?"

"Uh, hey, April!" he answered casually, despite the situation he found himself in. "So, I'm kind of, uh, trapped inside this giant worm thing. It's cool. I'm alive and stuff . . ."

Inside the Kraathatrogon, purple coils wrapped themselves around Casey tightly.

"You're *inside* the worm?" April asked. "You get a signal in there?"

"It's, uh, trying to digest me, I think," Casey said, straining to talk. "Could use . . . a little help . . ."

"Sit tight, Casey!" April said. "I mean, um, don't go anywhere!"

She covered her phone with her hand and turned to Donnie. "He's alive! He's ALIVE!"

CHAPTER 21

Leo stealthily climbed up the outside of Shredder's lair, his two *katana* swords strapped to his shell. He pulled out three sharp throwing stars when he reached the top of a spire and hurled them at one of the Footbots standing guard. The stars neatly lopped off his mechanical head.

As the other Footbot looked at the guard's fallen head, Leo flipped over him, landed at his feet, and swiped his swords at the bot's legs. The machine fell, and Leo slammed his swords down on it, dismantling it completely.

Leo climbed up a wall and slipped into the lair through a broken window. He immediately spotted his sensei lying on the ground unconscious and quickly made his way down to the floor to get close to Splinter.

"Sensei!" Leo whispered. Splinter didn't stir. Leo repeated the term of respect a little louder: "Sensei!"

Splinter's eyes slowly opened. He looked up to see his son. "Leonardo!" He managed to lift his chin a few inches from the floor. "Go! NOW!"

But it was too late for Leo to escape. All around the hall, torches burst into flame, lighting the chamber for the battle between Shredder and Splinter.

Shredder stepped into the hall with Karai and saw the Turtle. Leo tried to draw his *katana,* but Tiger Claw was suddenly right behind him and grabbed his arm. Behind the assassin stood Rahzar, Fishface, and Baxter Stockman. Leo struggled to get free, but Tiger Claw held him tight.

"Hello again, my friend," Tiger Claw purred in a low voice.

Shredder leaned in and demanded, "Where are the *other* Turtles?"

Tiger Claw sniffed the air. "It's just him, Master

Shredder. He's alone—I sense no one else."

Leo glared at Shredder, but the villain wasted no more time on the young Turtle. He turned and walked swiftly to Splinter, who still lay on the stone floor. Shredder shot the blades out of his wrist armor and cut Splinter's chains.

"Watch, Turtle, for it will be the last fight you ever see . . . the destruction of your master, Hamato Yoshi!"

Leo struggled to break loose from Tiger Claw's powerful grasp.

Splinter shook his head, trying to shake off the effects of the poison that lingered in his system. He assumed a martial arts stance, but his vision was blurred. He blinked, trying to clear his eyes.

Shredder pounced, thrusting the long blades that extended from his hands at Splinter. The poisoned rat managed to slip away, dodging three blows and a flying kick.

"You can do it, Sensei!" Leo called.

But it was a struggle for Splinter just to stay on his feet. Shredder came whirling at him, catching him with his armored knee and sending the sensei flying, landing on the hard stone floor with a loud *whump*!

"Sensei!" Leo cried, desperate to help his master. Tiger Claw let out a cruel, pitiless laugh.

High above them, on a ledge just inside the broken window, Raph and Mikey peered down at the fight. Mikey held a few of his favorite fireworks in his hands.

Groaning and gasping, Splinter managed to get to his feet and raise his arms. Karai looked at the ground, unable to watch.

Shredder rushed at Splinter, easily knocking him to the ground. He reached down and lifted the rat. Holding him with one arm, he drew back his other arm, aiming the twin blades at Splinter's head. "I will put you out of your misery."

But before Shredder could strike, another earthquake shook the city. The glass in the lair's roof cracked. Shredder dropped Splinter and staggered back, trying to regain his balance.

Lying on the ground, Splinter noticed a crack forming in the glass covering a pool of water below. He summoned all his strength and struck the crack. It raced across the glass, breaking beneath Shredder's feet! Weighed down by his heavy armor, he plunged into the pool of water!

At the same moment, strings of firecrackers, bottle rockets, and other explosives started to go off inside the hall. Leo took advantage of the diversion and broke free of Tiger Claw's grip.

Up on the ledge, Mikey put his fists in the air and took a couple of joyful steps from side to side. "Awwww, yeah! Rescue time!"

He and Raph jumped down into the action. Together the three Turtles stood in front of their master, guarding him.

"GET THEM!" Tiger Claw commanded.

BOOM! One last firework burst, filling the lair with blinding sparks and stars!

When the smoke cleared, the Turtles and their master were gone.

"NOOOO!" Tiger Claw bellowed.

Shredder hauled himself out of the pool. Fishface ran over to him. "Master Shredder!"

Shredder shoved the purple mutant aside. "Do not let them escape, fools! GO!"

On a nearby rooftop, the Turtles were moving as fast as they could, but it wasn't easy. They had to drag and carry Splinter.

Shaking his head, Splinter said, "You were foolish to come for me."

"We'd never leave you, Sensei," Raph said as he and Leo carried Splinter between them across the roof.

Donnie and April ran through the maze of old subway tunnels looking for the one where they last encountered the Kraathatrogon. When they reached the intersection of two tunnels, Donnie held up his hand, signaling for April to stop. "This is it!" he said with certainty. "This is the tunnel."

He pulled his *bo* staff off his back and walked toward the metal tracks. "Great," April said. "Now what?"

Donnie started whacking the metal rail with his staff. *TWHANG! TWHANG! TWHANG!* "I'm creating a vibration that'll attract the worm!"

April looked skeptical. "You really think a *stick* is gonna attract the . . ." She stopped talking and gasped. The huge worm was thumping down the track straight toward them! It opened its mouth and roared!

"The satchel!" Donnie said. April opened the leather satchel she was carrying and looked inside for the first time. She was expecting to see a powerful weapon they could use against the gigantic worm. Instead, she saw containers of . . . salt.

"Salt?"

"Salt's ionic strength can burn through a worm's neurosecretory cells! It's like . . . acid!"

"Yeah, but . . . SALT?"

The worm was moving faster now, rushing down the tracks like a roaring locomotive. Donnie held his *bo* staff like a baseball bat. April lobbed one of the salt containers, and Donnie batted it straight at the worm.

The container burst against the Kraathatrogon's head. And the giant worm . . . kept on coming!

April kept lobbing the salt containers to Donnie, and he kept batting them with his *bo* staff.

He never missed! He sent every container of

salt flying straight at the huge worm, spraying salt all over its head and mouth.

But the worm kept on barreling down the tunnel!

Finally, April said, "Uh, Donnie? We're out!"

She showed him the empty satchel.

And the worm *still* kept coming. . . .

"No, wait!" Donnie said, reaching into his pocket. He pulled out Jack Kurtzman's saltshaker—the one that had given him the salt idea in the first place.

He waited until the worm got a little closer, and then he hurled the glass saltshaker. It shattered on the rails, spraying a cloud of salt.

April bravely ran up to the spilled salt and waved her sharp-edged fan, raising a bigger cloud of salt.

The worm heaved its body forward, pulse by pulse, until it passed through the salt cloud. Finally, it came to a stop right in front of Donnie and April, breathing heavily.

"Huh?" Donnie said, wondering exactly what it was doing.

Then . . . *SPEW!* The worm opened its mouth and vomited out a tidal wave of green gunk, blasting April and Donnie back through the tunnel.

But when the flood of goo dissipated, they saw that the worm had also spewed out . . . Casey!

"CASEY!" April cried, hugging him, despite how slimy he was.

"April!" Casey said, feeling instantly better.

"Anybody have any hand sanitizer?" Donnie asked. Then he noticed that the wave of worm goo had washed them back into the mutagen-milking chamber . . . and there was something going on in there!

"Hate to break up the reunion," Donnie said to April and Casey, who were still hugging. "But we have big, huge, GIANT problems!"

April and Casey looked into the chamber and gasped! They saw several Kraang-droids pulling on cables, trying to wrangle another Kraathatrogon through the inter-dimensional portal. But this was the biggest one yet—the kind of huge adult Kurtzman had described. It must have been several hundred feet long!

"Now, that's a big worm," Casey said.

CHAPTER 23

Rahzar, Fishface, Karai, and Tiger Claw leaped across the rooftops of New York City, hunting the Turtles. Tiger Claw stopped and sniffed the night air. "I smell the reptiles!" He blasted forward with his jetpack.

Karai sprinted across a roof and leaped onto an elevator shaft for a higher vantage point. "If they escape, Shredder will have ALL your hides!" she warned.

"And what about *yours,* Karai?" Rahzar sneered.

On another roof, the Turtles had stopped to let Splinter rest. They knew they had to keep moving, but they were worried about him.

"I must get the poison out of my system," Splinter said haltingly.

Mikey handed him a gourd. "Drink some water, Sensei."

Splinter took the gourd gratefully and lifted it to his lips, taking a good, long sip of cool water. Then he handed the water gourd back to Mikey and said, "Must . . . meditate." He sat up, closed his eyes, and pressed his index fingers together in front of his nose, bowing his head.

"Let him rest," Raph said, standing up. "We'll keep a lookout for those goons."

He rounded the corner of the small building they were hiding behind and gasped! The goons were right there! Tiger Claw was in front, aiming his blaster at Raph.

Mikey and Leo came out and saw the members of the Foot Clan. "Heh heh," Mikey said. "Found 'em!"

"ATTACK!" Tiger Claw shouted. He blasted his jetpack, rising above the Turtles. Rahzar, Fishface, and Karai ran forward. Yelling, the three

Turtles sprang to meet their enemies. The rooftop battle was on!

Leo used his *katana* swords against Karai, knocking her back. Tiger Claw swung his wide blade at Leo, but the Turtle spun and blocked the blow with his sword.

Closing in on Raph, Fishface spun a gleaming, high-tech blade. "Fancy new weapon, Fishface!" Raph observed. "Let's see if ya know how to use it!"

"I'm going to chop you into tiny chucks and feed you to my piranha!" Fishface threatened, just before he ran at Raph.

Mikey jumped out of Rahzar's reach, using his parkour skills to bound off walls and pieces of equipment. "Too slow, Rahzar!" Mikey taunted.

Leo knocked Tiger Claw back, wheeled, and kicked Karai away. He turned back to Tiger Claw, and they slammed their swords together. "Your skills are *nothing* compared to mine," Tiger Claw jeered. "You are still just a cub!"

Tiger Claw knocked one of Leo's *katana* away. Leo parried the tiger-man's blows with the *katana* in his left hand. But Tiger Claw used his broad sword to pin Leo's *katana* to a wall and then *SLAMMED* his massive paw onto the sword, snapping it in two!

Tiger Claw roared a triumphant roar. But Leo quickly slipped a secret blade out of the handle of his broken *katana* and cut Tiger Claw's shoulder!

Shocked by Leo's maneuver, Tiger Claw fell back. Perhaps he had underestimated this Turtle. . . .

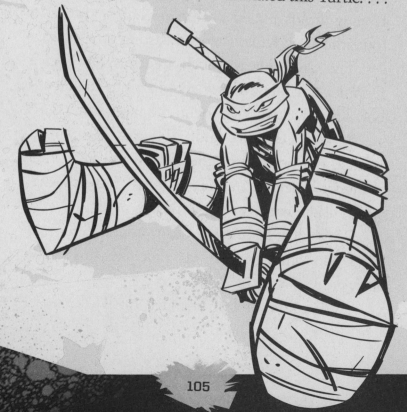

CHAPTER 24

In the huge mutagen-milking chamber, the Kraang-droids pulled on metal chains, trying to force the adult Kraathatrogon through the portal.

The droids were much too busy to notice Donnie, April, and Casey slipping into the chamber. They ducked down behind a large stone gear.

"Okay," Donnie said. "Here's the plan. I reverse the polarity of the portal and keep that thing from getting in." He pointed to the mechanisms at the very top of the portal.

"And what'll we do?" Casey asked.

"You guys create a diversion," Donnie answered.

"What kind of a diversion?" April asked.

"Leave that to Casey Jones!" Casey said, pointing to himself with tons of confidence.

Casey wasted no time. He jumped out into the open and yelled at the Kraang-droids, "Yo! Alien freak jobs!" He stuck his tongue out and blew a loud raspberry.

It certainly got the robots' attention. "It is humans, known as . . . humans," one droned in his metallic voice. He lifted a blaster and fired.

"I hope you have a plan other than getting shot at, Jones!" April said.

Donnie climbed up to a ledge that led to the top of the portal. With his back to the wall, he hoped the droids wouldn't notice him.

The battle on the rooftop raged on. As Raph and Fishface's weapons clanged, and Mikey taunted Rahzar, Splinter slowly came out of his meditative state.

Suddenly, he opened his eyes wide. He was back, the poison beaten.

Tiger Claw leaped into the air and raised his

right paw with all its sharp claws extended, ready to slash Leo. The Turtle covered his face with both arms, steeling himself for the pain. But the blow never came . . .

. . . because Splinter blocked it! Tiger Claw involuntarily let out a pathetic little meow of fear. Splinter grabbed the mutant's arm, spun him around, and twisted with both hands as he yanked Tiger Claw's arm toward the ground and let go. Tiger Claw went spinning across the roof!

"Now it is time to end this!" Splinter said in his strongest voice. His three sons ran to his side and embraced him.

Casey was thoroughly enjoying himself, using his hockey stick to slap hockey pucks at the Kraang-droids.

He knocked a hockey puck with a firework taped to it right into the hand of a Kraang-droid. The droid examined the hockey puck, saying, "Kraang detects inferior weaponry," just before the firework blew up and destroyed it.

The droids were so busy fighting April and Casey, they left the gigantic worm unattended. It writhed in the portal.

With the robots distracted, Donnie was able to climb his way up to the top of the portal. He found the main control box and yanked off its cover. Inside was a bewildering tangle of alien wires and strange devices. Reversing the polarity wasn't going to be easy.

Casey skated around the chamber, whacking droids with his hockey stick.

A Kraang-droid that had been knocked to the floor received an order: "Kraang, unleash another Kraathatrogon!" He raised himself up and slammed his metal fist against a control panel.

The milking harnesses fell away from one of the giant worms already in the chamber. Finding itself free, it rose up, opened its mouth, and showed its fearsome teeth!

April and Casey turned and saw the worm just as it dove toward them, letting out its sickening roar!

CHAPTER 25

Back on the roof, Splinter battled Tiger Claw. Raph fought Fishface. Mikey took on Rahzar. And Leo was defending himself from Karai.

"Karai! I don't want to fight you anymore! I'm not your enemy!"

Before she could answer, the building began to shake from all the worm action below the streets. Karai and Leo gasped. All the fighters swayed and stumbled, trying to regain their footing.

But as the shaking continued, Karai couldn't regain her balance. She staggered, tripped, and fell over the edge of the roof, screaming!

"KARAI!" Leo yelled as he tried to grab her foot before she fell. But he was too late.

"NOOO!" Splinter yelled. He ran to help his daughter, but Tiger Claw stamped his massive paw down on the rat's long tail. Splinter fell facedown on the ground.

The Kraathatrogon that was released from its harnesses raised the front of its heavy body up into the air for a moment, and then came crashing down! April and Casey leaped out of the way.

April stared at the worm lying in front of her. "I've got an idea! Something that Kurtzman said."

On the other side of the worm, Casey got to his knees and looked up. A Kraang-droid was standing right over him, aiming its blaster.

Just as the Kraang-droid was about to fire . . . The worm knocked the robot away!

Casey looked up and saw . . . April! She was *riding* the worm! She patted the worm and offered Casey her hand, saying, "Come on, Jones!"

Casey took her hand and scrambled up the side of the worm. When he lifted his hand off its back, his hand was covered in the worm's sticky goo. But even if it was gross, Casey felt pretty safe on the back of the giant worm.

April grabbed the worm's antennae and jerked them. "Hyaah! Move it, girl!" The worm plowed right into a crowd of Kraang-droids blasting their weapons. It knocked them down like bowling pins. "Go, worm, GO!" April whooped.

She steered the worm below the portal to where Donnie was struggling to reverse the polarity. Casey called up, "We'll distract the Kraang!"

"Do your thing, Donnie!" April added.

"I don't believe it," Donnie said to himself, amazed to see April and Casey riding the huge worm.

April steered the worm toward a subway tunnel. As it passed, it sent a cluster of Kraang-droids flying with just a flip of its tail. "To the surface, wormie!" April shouted.

"You are mine now, Yoshi-san!" Tiger Claw growled, pulling back his sword, ready to deal Splinter a deadly blow.

BAP! A small chunk of concrete hit Tiger Claw on the side of the head. In a rage, he turned to see who had thrown it at him. "Who dares?"

"HYAAAAAAAH!" Leo called out as he flew through the air straight at Tiger Claw, his foot extended in front of him. *WHAM!*

"OOOWAAH!" Tiger Claw grunted as he received the tremendous kick and flew over the edge of the roof, landing in a heap on a fire escape.

Leo dropped to Splinter's side. He heard a sound nearby and saw that Karai had climbed back up onto the roof, having landed on a ledge, unhurt. She looked away, unable to hold Leo's gaze.

Leo turned his attention back to his sensei. Splinter put his hand on his son's shoulder and said, "Not . . . too shabby." Leo smiled.

CRASH! Right next to the building, a Kraathatrogon smashed through the street from the subway tunnel below and reached all the way up to the roof!

But what was even more surprising to Leo and Splinter was who was *riding* the enormous worm! "WHOO-HOOOOO!" April whooped.

"YESSS!" Casey shouted.

Splinter and Leo just stared.

So did Mikey and Rahzar.

And Raph and Fishface.

But Tiger Claw didn't stare. Still breathing hard from Leo's tremendous kick, he fired up his jetpack and flew back up onto the roof. He zoomed toward Splinter, swinging his broad sword.

Splinter dodged the stroke of the sword and

immediately went on the attack, punching Tiger Claw in the face, then swiftly chopping him in the chest three times. Finally, Splinter spun all the way around and delivered a powerful kick that sent Tiger Claw flying into the air!

Tiger Claw fired up his jetpack, but he couldn't gain control of his flight. Spiraling and tumbling head over paws, he fell straight into the wide-open mouth of the gigantic worm! *"YAAAAHHHHH!"* he screamed as he disappeared into the beast.

Donnie was still at the portal's control box, feverishly working. "Gotta reverse the polarity," he muttered to himself. *But how?*

He tried a different configuration of the controls and looked up to see if the portal changed. It wavered, squeezing the gigantic worm still trapped halfway through the inter-dimensional gate. Suddenly . . .

SPEW! The worm blew gunk out of its huge mouth!

Not exactly the result Donnie was hoping for.

"Work!" he said. "Why won't you work?"

He tried a new connection. The portal made a different sound, one that seemed as though it were sucking everything back in. *WHOOSH!* The enormous worm disappeared back through the portal!

"Ha! I did it! I rule!" Donnie whooped.

The Kraang-droids looked up at the portal, alarmed. The pulling force of the reversed portal sucked them in, along with the huge worm still in the chamber!

Donnie secured himself to the outside of the portal with strong cables so he wouldn't be sucked in. He had no interest in returning to Dimension X. . . .

The force of the reversed portal was so strong that it pulled the biggest worm back down from the surface, all the way through the subway tunnels—along with April and Casey! They fell off the worm, screaming, *"YAAAAHHHH!"*

The last worm was rapidly sucked through to Dimension X. When he saw April and Casey being pulled toward the opening, Donnie grabbed his *bo* staff and held it out in front of the portal for them to grab.

They came hurtling toward the spinning vortex. . . .

Casey managed to grab the staff with one hand. But April flew by him!

Just before she was sucked into the portal, April grasped Casey's gym shoe, holding on for dear life! Clutching his staff with one hand, Donnie reached up behind him and yanked wires out of the portal's control box. It powered down. Donnie flipped his staff with both hands, and Casey and April went flying back into the chamber, landing on the floor with a thump.

April lay there for a moment, stunned. Then she opened her eyes and looked around. Everything was quiet. The worms were gone, and the portal to Dimension X was closed.

Casey looked at April, smiled his gap-toothed smile, and gave her a thumbs-up.

Donnie ran over to see if they were okay. April

threw her arms around him and gave him a big hug, and he smiled a big gap-toothed smile of his own. "You did it, Donnie!" she said. "You saved the city!"

"I take back every bad thing I said about you, Donnie," Casey said, grinning. "You rule!"

The two rivals bumped fists.

CHAPTER 27

As the sun rose over New York City, the four Teenage Mutant Ninja Turtles reunited on the rooftop where the night's battle had taken place. Splinter stood at the edge of the roof, taking in the beautiful sunrise.

The Turtles were catching up on what each group had done, filling in the blanks. "So the earthquakes were caused by giant worms that lived under the sewers?" Raph asked. "That sounds worse than giant cockroaches!"

"But I'm stoked you guys are back," Mikey said, grinning. "C'mere!" He ran over and squeezed Donnie, Casey, and April together in a big hug. They laughed.

"We're glad to be back," Donnie said.

Leo smiled and walked over to Splinter, who was standing away from the happy group with his hands behind his back. "You did it, Sensei," Leo told him.

Leo peered over the edge of the roof. A crowd gathered down on the street to gawk at the huge hole left by the worm when it had smashed up from the old subway tunnel. Several police cars were parked at the scene, and the police had cordoned off the gaping hole.

"With the help of my brave sons," Splinter answered. He turned and looked at the others proudly. "Yes. We *all* did it."

"But what about Karai?" Raph asked, walking over to Splinter and Leo.

"I still can't believe that evil witch is your daughter," April said, joining them. Then she realized what she had said. "Um, sorry to be so honest," she apologized.

Nearby, up on the catwalk behind a huge billboard, Karai sat, listening.

"Perhaps one day she will believe the truth," Splinter said. "But that is her decision."

Karai looked troubled. She didn't know what to think. Part of her believed Splinter truly was her father. But she still wasn't sure how she felt about that. . . .

"For now," Splinter continued, "we celebrate."

"Yay-uh!" Mikey agreed as they all headed off the roof. "Time for one of Antonio's pizza!" He stopped then, having thought of a question. "So, where do you think those space worms went, anyway?"

In a strange dimension, flat-looking people walked along the street. It was the world the Turtles had glimpsed through one of the magenta pyramids earlier in the day—the one where they looked like dorky cartoon characters!

High above the street, the four cartoony Turtles sat on a roof, eagerly eating cheesy pizza. Suddenly, a blue light flashed in the street below. An inter-dimensional portal opened, and a gigantic worm came through it!

Cartoon Leo pointed down at the worm. "Hey! Do you guys see that?"

"Whoa, dudes!" cried Cartoon Mikey. "A giant freaky worm! Totally mondo bizarro!"

People screamed as they ran away from the worm, which now looked flat and cartoonish, just like everything else in this strange dimension.

"I bet that pesky Shredder and Kraang are

behind this!" Cartoon Donnie said.

Cartoon Raph nudged Cartoon Leo. "You know what that means, right, Leo?"

Cartoon Leo got a determined look on his face. "We take down the creepy crawler . . . and then we order more PIZZA!"

They all jumped to their feet and spun their weapons.

"YES!" Cartoon Donnie cried. "TURTLE POWER!"

They leaped off the building to go fight the worm. As they dropped toward the street, they all yelled, *"BOOYAKASHA!"*